Doc Around the Clock

SPIDER-MAN 2

COLUMBIA PICTURES PRESENTS A MARVEL ENTERPRISES/LAURA ZISKIN PRODUCTION
TOBEY MAGUIRE "SPIDER-MAN® 2" KIRSTEN DUNST JAMES FRANCO ALFRED MOLINA ROSEMARY HARRIS DONNA MURPHY
MUSIC BY DANNY ELFMAN EXECUTIVE PRODUCERS STAN LEE KEVIN FEIGE EXECUTIVE PRODUCER JOSEPH M. CARACCIOLO BASED ON THE MARVEL COMIC BOOK BY STAN LEE AND STEVE DITKO
SCREEN STORY BY ALFRED GOUGH & MILES MILLAR AND MICHAEL CHABON SCREENPLAY BY ALVIN SARGENT PRODUCED BY LAURA ZISKIN AVI ARAD DIRECTED BY SAM RAIMI

MARVEL

sony.com/Spider-Man

DISTRIBUTED BY COLUMBIA TRISTAR FILM DISTRIBUTORS INTERNATIONAL

Spider-Man 2: Doc Around the Clock

First published in the USA by HarperFestival in 2004
First published in Great Britain by HarperCollinsEntertainment in 2004
HarperCollinsEntertainment is an imprint of HarperCollins*Publishers* Ltd,
77-85 Fulham Palace Road, Hammersmith, London W6 8JB

135798642
ISBN 0-00-717818-2

Printed and bound by Scotprint

www.harpercollinschildrensbooks.co.uk
www.sony.com/Spider-Man

Prologue

You don't expect that your whole life is going to change in just one day. Usually things happen slowly, a little bit at a time. How can you possibly think that you're going to be one thing, one person, on one day . . . and the next day, twenty-four hours later, you're someone and something completely different from how you started.

This book covers twenty-four

hours—one day—in the life of a man who started out as a very good man. He was a scientist. He had friends. He wasn't much different from you or your parents or teachers. All he really wanted to do was help people.

Then things went wrong. Terribly wrong. By the next day, he was a villain, a bad guy. Everyone was afraid of him, and he was perfectly happy about that. Not only that, but he wanted to destroy a man who was one of the best and bravest people in the city: none other than the amazing Spider-Man.

Who would want to do such a thing? Well, when he began his day, he was called Dr. Otto Octavius. But one day later, when he was scaring the entire city of New York, he came to be known as . . . Doc Ock.

This is his story.

1:00 P.M. TO 3:00 P.M. Chapter 1

Dr. Otto Octavius wasn't at all nervous, but Harry Osborn was.

Harry Osborn was the head of special projects at a company called OsCorp. OsCorp tried to come up with machines that would make people's lives better, but lately OsCorp had been having a lot of money troubles. Harry had spent a lot of money backing Dr. Octavius's new invention . . .

and he wasn't even entirely sure what it was. Dr. Octavius was keeping it hidden under a big sheet in the corner of his laboratory.

Scientists were coming into the laboratory and taking their seats. Harry had invited them there because Dr. Octavius had told him he was ready to show everyone his new invention. "Can't you show me first? After all, I paid for it!" said Harry. But Dr. Octavius wouldn't budge.

"Don't worry about it, Harry," said Harry's best friend, Peter Parker. Peter was a college science student and had known Harry since they were in high school.

(What Harry didn't know was that two years earlier, Peter had been bitten by a genetically altered spider while visiting a museum exhibit, and that bite had given Peter the powers of a spider. He could climb walls, spin webs, and

he was very fast and had great strength. He used these powers to fight crime as Spider-Man, but he made sure to keep that part of his life a secret.)

"I am worried, Peter," said Harry. "If Otto's invention doesn't work, OsCorp will be out of money. How will I pay the bills?"

"Dr. Octavius is a genius. If he says it'll work, it'll work," Peter told him. Even as he spoke, though, Peter was concerned. What if something did go wrong?

At that moment, Dr. Octavius gathered all the scientists together and pulled a sheet off his invention. No one knew what to make of it. It had four long metal "arms" that looked like tubes, with large pincers for grabbing at each end. They attached on the back of a harness, which Dr. Octavius strapped onto himself.

"I call them my 'smart arms'!" he announced. "They can do anything my brain tells them to do! One doctor could perform an operation all by himself instead of needing people to help him. A police officer would never have to worry about being outnumbered by members of a gang."

At first the arms just hung there, unmoving. But then Dr. Octavius switched them on, and the arms came to life.

The scientists gasped in amazement as the

Doc Around the Clock

Adaptation by Jacob Ben Gunter
Based on the Motion Picture
Screenplay by Alvin Sargent
Screen Story by
Alfred Gough & Miles Millar
and Michael Chabon
Based on the Marvel Comic Book by
Stan Lee and Steve Ditko

HarperCollins
Entertainment

SPIDER-MAN 2

arms moved around like giant metal snakes. In the middle of them stood Dr. Octavius. He kept talking about how useful his smart arms would be. Harry had a huge grin on his face, thinking about all the money that could be made from selling the smart arms to hospitals, police departments, and many other organizations.

But Peter noticed that the arms were starting to act strangely. They whipped back and forth, and Dr. Octavius didn't seem completely in control of them. "Harry, maybe you should tell him to shut them down," said Peter.

"Are you kidding?" said Harry. "It's a total success! This is the greatest day of my life!"

Suddenly one of the arms shot straight up and crashed into the ceiling. Huge chunks of debris fell from overhead. People in the audience shouted in alarm and started running for the exits.

"Wait! Come back!" yelled Harry Osborn as the smart arms continued to flail about, tearing into the walls and knocking over machinery. Even Peter Parker was gone, having been one of the first out the door. Harry turned to Otto Octavius and pointed at him angrily. "This is your fault! This invention was supposed to make me a ton of money! You've ruined everything!"

Dr. Octavius had no idea what was going

wrong with the arms. They were moving in all directions as if they'd developed minds of their own. But the one thing he was sure of was that he didn't like Harry yelling at him.

The arms didn't seem to like it, either. Harry yelped in alarm as several of the arms shot toward him, looking as if they were ready to tear him apart.

Suddenly Harry was flying through the air. He found, to his shock, that Spider-Man had shown up. He didn't know, of course, that Spider-Man was his friend Peter, who had run out and changed into his costume. All he knew was that Spider-Man was hauling him out of the room as fast as he could.

The moment Spider-Man had Harry in the clear, he turned to face Dr. Octavius.

Unfortunately, Dr. Octavius had been reading all the articles in the *Daily Bugle,* the newspaper that was always lying about Spider-Man, saying he was actually a crook. "You must have done this!" said Dr. Octavius. "You did something to my smart arms."

"No, I didn't!" Spider-Man said, but Dr. Octavius wasn't listening. The arms swept at Spider-Man, as if they were reflecting the doctor's anger. Spider-Man dodged them, and one of the arms slammed into an electrical generator.

Thousands of volts of electricity crashed through the arms and into Dr. Octavius himself. Dr. Octavius screamed, his whole body shaking. Spider-Man quickly yanked out the power cord from the smart arms machine. The moment the power was cut off, Dr. Octavius fell over and his smart arms went limp.

Spider-Man tried to remove the harness from Dr. Octavius's body. But the doctor had been hit with so much electricity that the harness had practically melted right onto his body.

"He's going to have to go to the hospital," muttered Spider-Man. "I hope they can help him there."

Chapter 2

3:00 P.M. TO 6:00 P.M.

Dr. Isaacs was one of the best surgeons at Booth Memorial Hospital, but even he had never seen anything like what had happened to Dr. Octavius.

The famous scientist was lying facedown on a table in the middle of the largest operating room in the hospital. His smart arms—which many people were calling "tentacles," as if Octavius were a

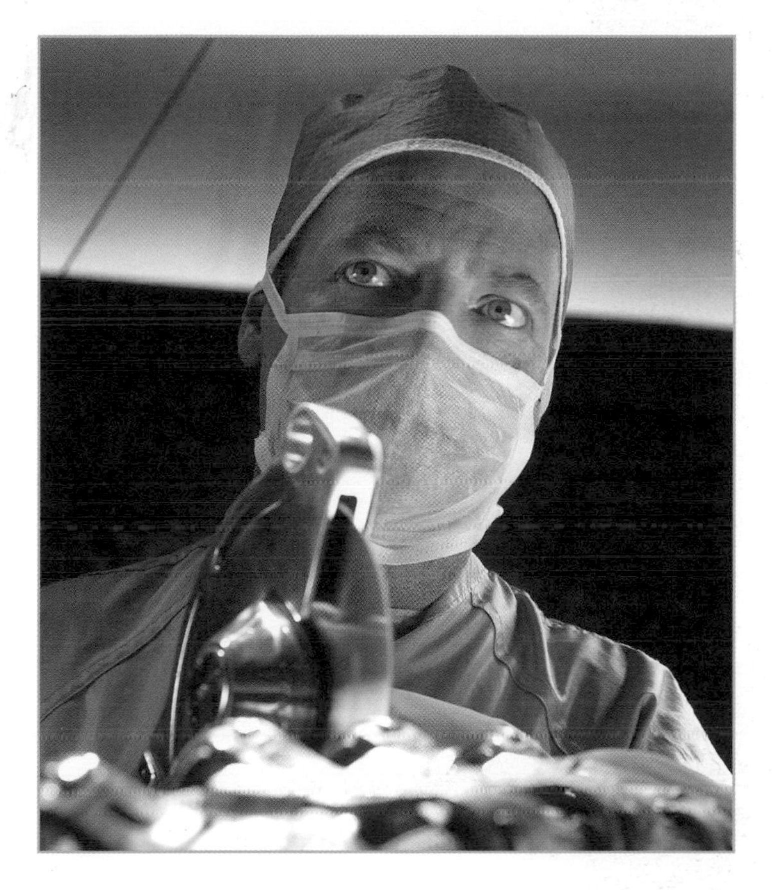

giant octopus—were draped in cloth so the dirt from them wouldn't get germs in the operating room.

The nurses and the other doctors who were going to assist in the operation looked on in amazement as Dr. Isaacs studied his patient

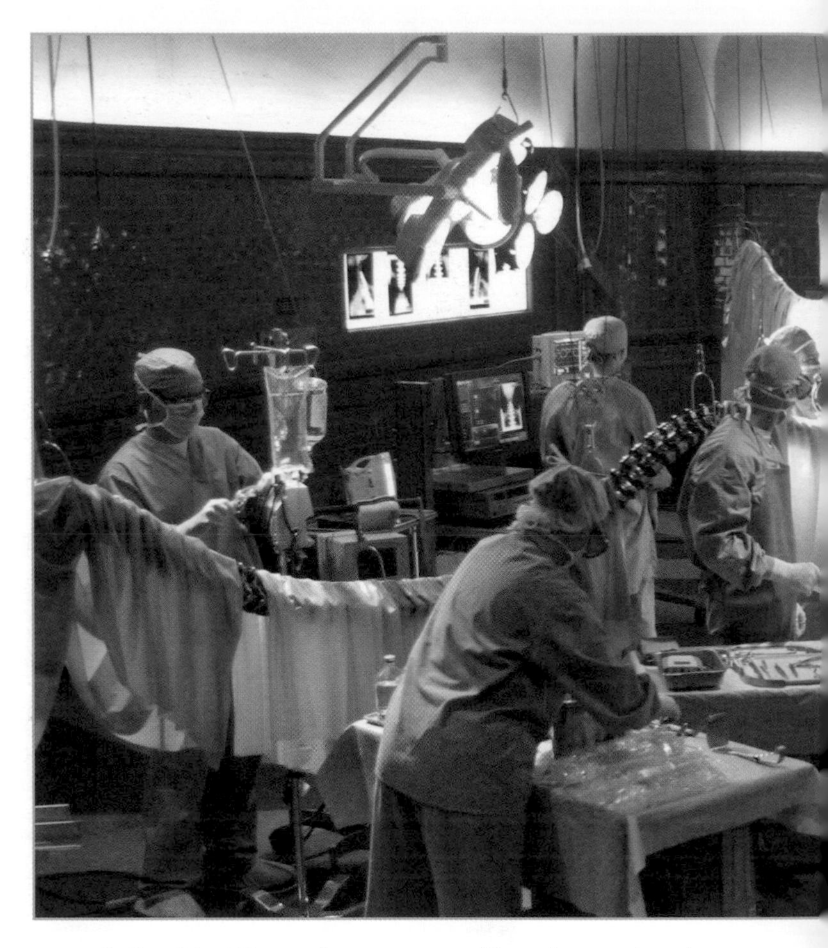

carefully. Dr. Octavius was still asleep, having been knocked out by the powerful electricity. The tentacles, which had been so fearsome hours earlier, were limp and lifeless.

"We're going to have to cut the harness

off," Dr. Isaacs finally announced. "There's no other way to do it."

After making sure that Dr. Octavius wouldn't wake up anytime soon, Dr. Isaacs prepared to remove the harness. He took a small circular saw and started it up.

He didn't notice the tentacles beginning to twitch, as if in response to the noise of the saw.

Dr. Isaacs knew that, in cutting off the harness, he'd basically be destroying the arms. But he figured that shouldn't be too much of a problem. The arms were just machines, after all. It wasn't as if they were going to do anything about it.

As it turned out, he was wrong.

Out of the corner of his eye, he thought he caught some sort of movement. He hesitated, the buzz saw barely an inch above the harness, about to make the first cut. "What was that?" he asked and looked where he thought he had seen something moving around.

To his shock, one of the tentacles suddenly ripped right up and angled toward Dr. Isaacs,

who stayed right where he was, paralyzed in shock.

The tentacle grabbed the buzz saw and crushed it in its large pincers. Dr. Isaacs barely got his hand away in time; if he hadn't, he would have seen it get mashed along with the surgical tool.

He stumbled back over his own feet. The tentacle grabbed him by the front of his surgical

gown and threw him across the operating room. He collided with an equipment table on the far side and slumped to the floor, unconscious.

The other tentacles broke free from their anchors as well. Just as the scientists had been scrambling to get out of the laboratory earlier, now the doctors and nurses were trying to get out of the operating room. The tentacles wouldn't let them go. It was as if they wanted to punish the hospital staff for threatening them.

They knocked the doctors and nurses this way and that, as if they were hockey pucks. People skidded in one direction, tumbled in another. In seconds, the only things moving in the room were the tentacles. Every human being in the place was knocked out cold.

That included Dr. Octavius himself. He was still lying on the table, unmoving, unaware of everything that had happened to him. The arms circled him and started nudging him, poking at him until finally he sat up. He looked up and stared around the operating room. At first he didn't understand what he was seeing. Then, slowly, it began to dawn on him.

"What have I done?" he cried out. He looked accusingly at the arms and said, "What have *you* done?"

Then he saw the ruined buzz saw on the floor. "They were going to destroy you," he muttered. "Destroy my greatest creation. How could they even think of doing such a thing!"

The electricity had literally fried his mind. Dr. Octavius wasn't capable of thinking straight. Instead his thoughts focused on who was jealous of him, who wanted to do him harm. He was starting to see enemies everywhere, including the people who only cared about helping him.

"We've got to get out of here," he said. All he had to do was think it, and the arms immediately responded. They reached over toward the nearest wall and tore into it. They tossed brick and mortar around, taking care so that none of it hit Dr. Octavius. The moment a path was clear, the arms lifted Octavius up and out of the hospital.

He found an old trench coat lying in a Dumpster and draped it around himself for warmth and protection against the fierce rain pouring from overhead.

Then he wandered away into the streets of Queens, still dazed and confused but also burning with slowly growing anger.

Chapter 3

6:00 P.M. TO 9:00 P.M.

The police department went over the destruction in the hospital, trying to figure out what in the world had happened. The doctors and nurses were beginning to regain consciousness and were all too anxious to tell the incredible tale of the unconscious man and his powerful mechanical arms.

In the meantime, Dr. Otto Octavius was walking the streets,

heading in the general direction of his laboratory. Night was beginning to fall, and he drew the coat closer around himself. The tentacles also drew tighter around him.

"Well, well . . . what've we got here?"

There were several young men blocking his way, all wearing bloodred jackets. It was clear, even to the doctor's confused mind, that these were members of a street gang. One of them had a knife out and was pointing it in Otto's direction.

"Give us your money," said the largest one.

"Money. It's always about money, isn't it," mused Dr. Octavius. He sounded as if he were talking to himself, as if the gang members weren't even there. "Osborn's worried about money. And Spider-Man . . . well, he probably wants to be famous so he can have money, too."

The gang members looked at each other in confusion. "What're you wasting time for?" one of the shorter gang members asked the one with the knife. "Just cut him and take whatever he's got on him."

The one with the knife nodded and came right at Dr. Octavius. The doctor didn't move. He didn't have to. Instead, two of the tentacles abruptly slithered out from beneath the coat. "He's got some sort of snakes under there!" the one with the knife shouted, and then, with a single sweep, a tentacle sent him flying. He landed ten feet away, crashing through the canvas roof of a convertible.

A second gang member started to reach into his jacket for a gun. But before he could get the weapon clear, another tentacle had reached out, snatched the gun away, and crushed it in its pincers. The tentacles were so strong that they didn't need any weapons.

Two of the tentacles picked up the man who had tried to shoot them and lifted him high in the air. Then they shook him violently, so hard his teeth were rattling.

The other two gang members had seen more than enough by that point. "It's the octopus guy!" one of them cried out. "The one the cops are after! Let's get out of here!" And with that, they were sprinting down the street, leaving their fellow gang member behind to Otto's mercy.

"Please let me go!" howled the one being shaken, and the tentacles tossed him aside as if he were a rag doll. He landed headfirst in a trash can, which then toppled over. He didn't move for a long while after that.

Dr. Octavius watched the entire thing as if it were happening to someone else. At first he had been afraid of what these amazing arms attached to his back could do. Now, though, he was beginning to enjoy the power they gave him.

He turned away and continued walking toward his lab. All the way, he kept thinking about what that one thug had said.

"'The octopus guy. The one the cops are after,'" he said softly. He looked around the lab, his face filled with sadness.

And then a voice came from overhead. "Dr. Octavius," it said. "I was hoping you'd come back here."

Dr. Octavius turned and, for some reason, wasn't all that surprised to see none other than Spider-Man perched on the wall.

"Everyone wants to help you, Dr. Octavius," said Spider-Man. "We know you're not well . . ."

"Not well?" Octavius grinned. "I've never felt better in my life. As for helping me . . . no one wants to help me. They want to help Dr. Octavius."

"But that's you," Spider-Man said.

Octavius shook his head. "Wrong. I'm not Dr. Octavius anymore. Call me . . . *Doc Ock*!"

With that, he sent the tentacles in four different directions. Each one grabbed a support beam at each side of the room. Spider-Man's head snapped back and forth as he suddenly realized what was about to happen. "This isn't

going to end nicely," he groaned.

The tentacles tore apart the support beams all at the same time, and the entire building started to collapse. Doc Ock wasn't worried. Two of the tentacles created a shield over his head, the falling chunks of wood and plaster bouncing off them and causing no damage. The other two tentacles were anchored down into the ground below, so when all the floors fell down, Doc Ock was left hanging in midair, supported by his tentacles.

Perched high above the fallen rubble, Doc Ock looked at the mess with satisfaction. He knew the dead body of Spider-Man was somewhere below him in the collapsed building. Good. With Spider-Man gone, he was one less thing for Doc Ock to worry about.

His arms carried him away from the site of the demolished laboratory. "So much for Spider-Man," he said and decided it was time to find himself a new place to live.

Long moments passed, and there was no sign of life in the ruins. Then slowly, finally, the rubble was shoved aside.

Beneath that rubble was Spider-Man. He had spun a web above himself just as the building fell upon him, and the webbing had caught most of the debris. Still, his costume had been badly torn up, and there was so much dust he felt like he was suffocating. He removed his mask so he could breathe easier.

"That was close. That was too close," he said.

In the distance he could hear the sounds of police sirens. He wasn't surprised. A collapsing building wasn't something that would go unnoticed. But he certainly didn't need the police showing up and seeing him with his costume shredded and his mask off.

Quickly he made his way up and out from

under the web that had saved his life. Then he sprinted toward the nearest wall, climbed up the side, and was gone from the scene before the police got there.

There would be no more searching for Doc Ock this night. He had to get back to his apartment and fix his costume . . . fast. Doc Ock could be up to practically anything, and Spider-Man was convinced that he was the only one who could stop him.

Not that he'd done such a great job so far.

9:00 P.M. TO MIDNIGHT

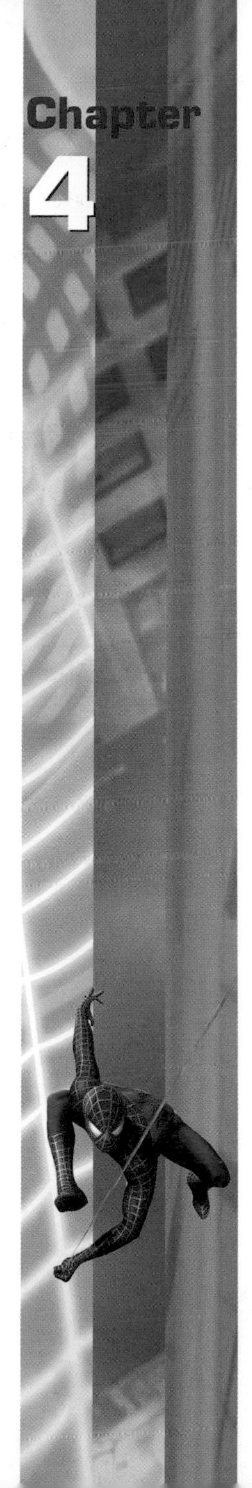

Doc Ock was able to cover great distances very quickly, thanks to the speed with which his tentacles could carry him. He used his arms to hitch a ride on the top of a passing commuter train, and within the hour, he had made it into the city.

Bright light of any kind hurt his eyes, so he had taken to wearing sunglasses. He knew he wanted someplace dark to hide in while he decided on his next step.

He found it when the arms brought him to a rotting old pier down by the docks. Pier 56, unused by boats for quite some time, was the perfect place.

But the fact that he was hiding at all angered him. After all, thanks to his mechanical arms, he was the most powerful person in New York . . . possibly in the entire world. He had beaten Spider-Man and had hardly broken a sweat doing it. If he could do that to Spider-Man, just imagine how easily he could dispose of any police officers who tried to stand in his way.

In a very short time, Doc Ock had found a warehouse on the pier that was clearly no longer in use. There he sat, watching the rats scuttle around. The rats in turn kept looking at him. But every time one of them would start to draw close, a tentacle would reach out, grab it, and squish it. The rats learned pretty quickly that staying away from Doc Ock was the best course of action.

Doc Ock was no longer thinking about Spider-Man, however. Instead he was dwelling on Harry Osborn. He hated to admit it, but he needed Osborn's help. Doc Ock had decided that the best thing to do was try to rebuild his laboratory . . . and that was going to take money. Lots of money.

Well, Harry Osborn certainly had that. He was the head of special projects at OsCorp and lived in a fancy townhouse in Manhattan. He probably had all the money that Doc Ock required, right in a safe at home.

Sitting in a dark warehouse at night was silly, Doc Ock reasoned, when Harry Osborn was in his fancy house, surrounded by his beloved money.

As far as Doc Ock was concerned, it was time to go tell Harry Osborn to share some money with him.

Midnight to 3:00 A.M.

Chapter 5

Harry Osborn sat alone in his townhouse, staring at the wall.

He had absolutely no idea what he was going to do. Harry couldn't believe that everything had fallen apart so quickly. Twelve hours ago, he had felt as if he were on top of the world. Dr. Octavius's invention was going to be one of the greatest gifts to mankind, ever. And OsCorp was going to

make a ton of money off it.

And now where was he? Dr. Otto Octavius was gone, and the newspapers—in fact, all New Yorkers—were calling him "Doc Ock." The police were out looking for him. Harry was getting angry calls from the scientists who had been there when the experiment had fallen apart. They were talking to their lawyers about suing him. Doc Ock had trashed the hospital, and now Harry had just gotten word that the laboratory where Doc Ock had first had his "accident" had been completely destroyed.

"What else could possibly go wrong?" Harry wondered out loud.

Suddenly there was a crash from Harry's balcony. He jumped to his feet and then let out a yell of alarm as he saw Doc Ock standing there, the wind billowing around him.

"Hello, Harry," said Doc Ock, as if they were the best of friends.

Harry started backing up, and he kept going until suddenly he was against the wall. "Wha—what do you want?" he stammered out.

"Money, Harry," Doc Ock told him. "And you're going to give it to me."

His hands trembling, Harry pulled out his wallet. "I've . . . I've got about a hundred dollars on me. . . ."

Doc Ock slapped the wallet away, annoyed. "I don't need small change. I need everything you've got. Everything and more."

"But I don't have much of anything here at all!" said Harry. "My money is all at the First National Bank over on Fifth Avenue. You can go rob it out of there!"

"Me?" said Doc Ock, and he grinned. "Why should I go to all that work when you can do it for me? Tomorrow, Harry, at twelve noon exactly. You will go to the bank and take out every single cent from each of your accounts.

And it had better be around five million dollars, or we're going to have some problems."

"Five . . . million?" Harry said with a gulp. But then he just nodded.

"And if I see any police officers there," Doc Ock warned him, "it won't go well for you."

"No police! I promise!" said Harry.

"See you tomorrow," said the villain, exiting with a crazed laugh.

Chapter 6

3:00 A.M. TO 11:00 A.M.

Peter Parker was up very late fixing his costume. By the time he finished, he could barely keep his eyes open.

He slumped back onto his bed, and immediately he began to dream. He saw himself as Spider-Man, captured by Doc Ock. Barbed wire was wrapped around his hands and feet, and Doc Ock was standing over him, smirking.

"Did you really think you could stop me, Spider-Man?" Doc Ock sneered at him.

Suddenly he wasn't Spider-Man anymore. Instead he was simply Peter Parker. Standing next to him was Mary Jane, his girlfriend, and Doc Ock was gripping him by the throat. "You can't get away from me," Doc Ock said. "Even in your dreams, I can still beat you with five arms tied behind my back."

"No," Peter managed to say, gasping, and then he woke up.

He sat up in bed, turned on the light, and just stared, becoming more and more nervous.

Doc Ock, meanwhile, was sleeping very soundly indeed. He was certain that everything was going to go exactly as he wanted. Why shouldn't it? He was completely in charge.

Peter went to class in the morning, but he

couldn't shake the nagging, growing feeling of fear. He stared down at his book for what seemed like ages, but he couldn't focus on the words at all.

I don't think I can beat him, he thought. *He's so powerful, and those tentacles of his just seem to come from every direction. They move faster than even I can dodge. They move as fast as he can think . . . maybe even faster.*

His thoughts were still whirling as he walked across the main campus. *What am I going to do, what am I going to do?* he kept asking himself. He knew that he was beating himself before he even got started, but he had no idea how to handle Doc Ock.

Peter was lost in thought when he heard a loud thump from nearby. He turned and saw that a jogger had plowed into a student who was walking in the opposite direction. The student's glasses were on the ground, and he grumbled in annoyance as he picked them up and tried to look through them. "They're all dirty!" he complained.

Peter's eyes went wide.

"That could work," he said, an idea beginning to grow in his head.

He thought he had a way to handle Doc Ock. Now all he had to do was find him . . . and Peter was having some thoughts about that as well.

11:00 A.M. TO 1:00 P.M.

Chapter 7

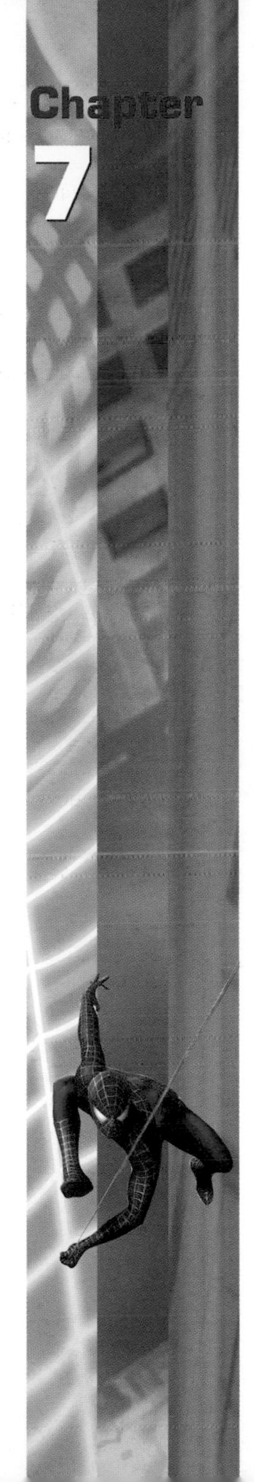

Harry Osborn walked into the First National Bank and looked around nervously. He was expecting to see Doc Ock waiting there, lurking in a corner. But he was nowhere to be seen.

Harry went over to one of the bank executives. The executive greeted him warmly, but then his face became very pale when Harry said he needed five million dollars.

“Mr. Osborn, you don’t have nearly that much in the bank,” he told him.

“I know,” said Harry. “Just give me however much I’ve got.”

And then a snickering voice said, “Don’t

worry about it. I've changed my mind."

Harry turned and saw, to his horror, that Doc Ock was standing right behind him.

"I've decided to take everything in the bank," said Doc Ock. "And you, Harry, get to watch."

The bank executive hit an alarm, but he was too late. The arms of Doc Ock lashed out and grabbed the door of the vault where most of the bank's money was kept. He ripped the door off its hinges, even though it was huge and made of steel.

A bank guard tried to pull out his gun, but one of the tentacles swung out and knocked the guard across the room.

Within minutes, Doc Ock had cleaned out the vault. Each of his tentacles was holding several large bags of money.

"You've got what you want!" said Harry Osborn. "Now just . . . just go!"

"Have a nice day, Harry," said Doc Ock, "and just think: You get to remember forever that you're responsible for all this."

Doc Ock headed out of the bank. As he walked outside, the police were pulling up. Using his tentacles, Doc Ock flipped the cars over, trapping the police inside.

"Hold on, Doctor!" a frustratingly familiar voice called from overhead. "We have some unfinished business!"

Doc Ock looked up and, sure enough, there was his greatest enemy. "Spider-Man!" he shouted. "How many times do I have to kill you?!"

"Only once, but you can't even manage that!" Spider-Man taunted him.

His tentacles speared toward Spider-Man, with actual spears popping out of the ends of the fearsome arms. "This is it, Spider-Man!"

"It sure is!" Spider-Man called back.

The tentacles came in fast and furious. Spider-Man dodged between them, moving so quickly that he was practically a blur. Then he was right on top of Doc Ock, and webbing was flying from his wrists as fast as he could spin it.

"What do you think you're doing?" Doc Ock shouted . . . and suddenly he couldn't see a thing. His glasses were completely covered with webbing.

He reached up with his own hands to try pulling the webbing off. Instead, all he succeeded in doing was getting his natural hands stuck to his face. He pulled and yelped as he almost tore the skin off his own head.

Doc Ock was effectively blinded by the webbing; he couldn't see anything. And if he was blind, so were his tentacles. They lashed about desperately, but they had no idea where Spider-Man was; no way of coming into contact with him, much less fighting him.

That was when Spider-Man came right at Doc Ock and hit him as hard as he could in the face. Doc Ock tumbled over, unconscious.

Within moments, Spider-Man had Doc Ock completely covered in webbing. He was tied so

tightly that even his powerful tentacles couldn't rip free.

"We'll take it from here, Spider-Man!" called out a police officer.

"Wait, you don't understand," said Spider-Man.

"We understand fine," another officer told him. "We've read all about you in the *Daily Bugle*. You're as bad as Doc Ock."

Spider-Man sighed heavily. "I'm sorry you believe that," he said, as he fired his webbing and swung upward.

And as he watched the officers throw Doc Ock's webbed-up body into a police van, he heard Doc Ock shout, "This isn't over, Spider-Man! Not by a long shot!"

Spider-Man would have liked to be sure that Doc Ock was wrong. Unfortunately, he wasn't. The only thing he was sure of was this: It had been a tough twenty-four hours.